THE
Little
Immigrant

THE
Little
Immigrant

By Corrado "Charlie" Ammatuna

The story of coming to America.

As told to

Lauren Snelgrove

edited by

Christina Hamlett

II

ISBN-10: 0-9839668-9-3

ISBN-13: 978-0-9839668-9-0

Published by

Providence Publications

P.O. Box 2610

Granite Bay, CA 95746

Library of Congress Control Number: 2013931864

Cover Design by Terry Ulick & Robbie Lynn

Design & Typography by Robbie Lynn

For Rosa,
my children
and for
immigrants everywhere

IV

Prologue

Who is this man Charlie Ammatuna – the one I kept hearing about and kept being told I had to meet? All I knew is that our boys carpooled to high school together sometimes. Who is this man who chose to be known as "Charlie I'm a tuna" in a country that eats Starkist? He had to be funny. I couldn't wait to meet him.

When I met Charlie it was after he was diagnosed with that horrid cancer called Mesothelioma and he knew the ultimate outcome. The outcome was clear although the time frame was not.

I remember that meeting him that first time was like seeing an old friend again. We were instant fast friends – close friends almost from the first minute. What an experience.

The voice and accent sounded like the TV comedian Father Guido Sarducci. All those Italian old country adjectives and allegories were a delight to listen to.

I once asked him how Corrado became Charlie. He got that slightly mischievous twinkle in his eye and said, "it just fit." I knew then it was partly his little joke on the rest of us. He was having fun with us.

"What do you do?" he asked me when we met. "I'm a CEO," I said, "How about you?"

"I'm a machinist." It was much later that we talked about his amazing career. He was a senior manager of several very large machine shops. Now when someone asks me, I say, I'm a journalist.

From Charlie we learned about humility.

Once when he was in the hospital I went to visit him. I walked into the room "Hi Charlie. How are you?"

"How are you," he said and made sure I answered. He peppered me with so many questions I didn't know if I was the house entertainment, if he just didn't want to talk about his situation, or what. At a time when we were all concerned for him, he brushed himself aside and he showed his concern for the rest of us.

From Charlie we learned about caring for others and each other.

Whether it was out to dinner or over his wife Rosa's spinach and olive oil salads, Charlie made us laugh and feel good about the world and about ourselves.

With a twinkle in his eye he could get to the heart of any matter with humor… and with those old world adjectives that he made fit the situation perfectly. Charlie accepted us and made sure we felt that way.

Charlie showed us how to love each other.

On the Friday when the blunt news came from the doctors that there was no more that could be done and very little time, we were all … well, we couldn't deny seeing the sun setting in the west and

VIII

our hearts dropped.

I had just received back – a day earlier – what we figured was the final draft of Charlie's – of this -- book. Saturday morning it was printed out and labeled with "FINAL DRAFT FOR AUTHOR APPROVAL." I took it over for him to see to hold and to read.

While his wife and son were out of the room the talk turned serious. It was between two friends who knew and understood that time was short.

"The doctor told the truth," he said, "I'm glad I went."

"Everyone has to get on the train eventually and now it's my turn," he told me. "My job as a father is done. I see my kids and I know I have completed the mission. They are good and they will be fine. I worry about Rosa but she will be fine in time too. I am ready to get on the train." He meant what he said. Charlie demonstrated for us love of family.

And it was against this backdrop that he

took his family on a cruise.

He was clearly sick – as sick as I'd ever seen him. And yet, he was ready and excited to be off on another adventure at sea. "We're gonna celebrate it," he told me.

Charlie demonstrated faith and bravery.

Charlie modeled humility and caring. He modeled for us fun and funny. He showed us love of each other, and love of family. He showed us faith and bravery.

Charlie modeled for us – he showed us how to be – simply put – a good person.

We are blessed, each of us, for knowing him.

Let's celebrate with the story he wrote.

J Dale Debber

* * *

The sweet scent of chocolate and wine still lingered on our breaths that afternoon – a fusion of flavors which, even to this moment, always reminds me of home.

It was the day after Easter and, as tradition goes in the Gordini family, we were bustling around in preparation for a countryside picnic. "Have I packed too much?" my mother fretted aloud, prompting a laugh from the rest of us. My father Carlo, you see, drove a 1954 Topolino – practically a toy car! - built by the Fiat Motor Company. That a family of four could all squeeze into it was nothing less than a miracle. That a picnic basket brimming with food, a bundle of blankets and my sister Gina's favorite toys were going to share this cramped space, too – well, that was probably asking for <u>two</u> miracles!

"It's affordable," my father reminded us as he made a dramatic show of pretending that half of the food would need to be left at home on the sidewalk. Practicality was second nature to him; if the tiny Topolino – our "little mouse" could get us where we wanted to go, why should we want for something bigger?

I rolled my eyes, knowing that when I turned 16 the following year and wanted to drive, this is the very vehicle I'd be learning in. Perhaps by then, I mused, it would feel as grand to me as a limousine.

A warm sunshine gently embraced the Sicilian landscape around us, and a slight breeze whispered into the innocent ears of Gina and me. She was only three years old and such a source of astonishing wonder to me. Even when we were grown up, I imagined, I would still think of her as a baby. In typical sibling fashion, our impromptu game of front yard tag had culminated in my tickling her until she shrieked.

"Are you sure the two of you didn't leave anything behind in the house?" my mother softly asked for the second time in as many minutes.

"Sì mamma," I replied for the both of us. Gina only giggled and ran in dizzying circles around my legs. At this rate, I thought, she would be asleep before we ever got to our picnic.

"Corrado!" my father called out to me a moment later. "Have you checked the house?"

Anxious to set off, I quickly replied I had already checked – twice! - and that nothing was forgotten.

"What are we waiting for then?" he declared, proudly holding the passenger door open for Mama, his beloved co-pilot. Gina and I fought for space in the backseat, another favorite tradition of ours. Papa eased himself behind the wheel and, with that, we sped away for a day of glorious adventure and wonderful food.

Our country house wasn't but five miles from our hometown of Lessante. La Riviera - the road leading away from the house - was no easy drive, however, and its curves reminded me of a slithering snake. Could our little mouse of a car outrun it? I started to make up a story about it for Gina but by now she was singing a nonsensical song to her favorite doll and had no interest in paying attention to her older brother.

I turned my attention to the view outside the open windows. The crashing waves of the Mediterranean Sea lay to the left, and rich, lively vegetation devoured the mountainside to the right. Beauty surrounded us and I suddenly couldn't stop myself from talking up a storm about it. My parents exchanged a brief smile with one another in the front seat, no doubt wordlessly comparing how different I was from Gina.

Gina was more like my mother, I thought, and would grow up to be sweet, beautiful, kind and – unlike today – maybe even shy and quiet. I would be more like my father and be able to fix any problem. Mama said I already had his rugged good looks – albeit a scrawnier version - and his smile, a smile which she said was that of a "charmer". Character was all important to her, a fact she often reminded me of on the occasions when I attempted to charm my way out of chores around the house or explain to my teacher why I didn't finish my homework.

I had just started to say something about the picture-perfect weather that day. I can't remember exactly what it was. I only remember that we were approaching a sharp curve and that, for only a split-second, I saw a dog standing in the middle of the road. Papa tried to cut the wheels to the left to avoid hitting it. I also remember he tried to look back at Gina and me. Maybe it was to utter a word of reassurance that the dog had moved in just the nick of time.

Maria Ammatuna

Luigi Ammatuna

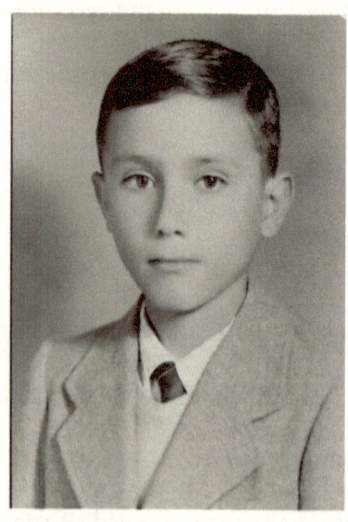

Corrado Ammatuna

His frantic maneuvering caused the car to lose control and commence a violent tumble over the rocky embankment and toward the sea. I tried to hold on to something – anything! – as we began our frightening descent. Jagged, alternating images of sky and water flashed before my eyes as my body was thrown like one of Gina's rag dolls from one side of the backseat to the other. Sounds – a scream, the shattering of glass, a crunch of metal – assailed my ears until everything all blended into something distant, hollow and unrecognizable.

And then…total silence.

The Topolino had come to a jolting and ungraceful halt on a fragile patch of land only a short drop from the menacing waters below. I blinked my eyes in disbelief, stunned by how precariously we seemed to hover above the waves. Terror had stolen anyone's ability to speak. No one screamed. No one cried. There was just one quiet gasp of relief that had come from my own mouth.

I slowly looked around, conscious that my quarters seemed smaller to me than when this trip had first begun. Just above, the ceiling was nearly touching my head. I would later be told that my scrawny frame had probably saved me from being crushed from the impact.

"Papa?" I murmured, inching forward as best as I could and realizing that there wasn't a part of my body that didn't hurt. I repeated his name but he didn't answer. And then I saw why.

A sheer black fright swept through me as I frantically looked toward the passenger seat. I tried to say her name but I knew that Mama, too, was beyond answering me – her body a mangled mess from the tiny car's collapse. How could Gina and I have lost both of them so quickly when we had all been laughing only a few minutes before?

Gina!

With the last bit of hope that had yet to be

drained from me, I turned my head. Like me, my little sister had escaped the compression of the roof but was slumped in shock against the seat, blood trickling from her mouth and ears, her beautiful brown eyes staring straight ahead but not seeing me. I fell forward, clenching my stomach, and threw up.

I could now feel the icy bite of glass on my skin. I could feel the tiny lacerations in my face and the blood trickling from what felt like a broken nose. Just below my right knee was a deep cut nearly four inches in length. The frame of the passenger seat in front of me had been the cause of my wound, the fabric ominously stained in my own blood.

Instinctively, I knew what I had to do. I knew my family needed help. I knew I needed to crawl out of the car and run and scream and pray to God for someone to find us and make us whole again. But I just couldn't move. I was still paralyzed from the moment, only wishing I could act on my thoughts. I looked towards my escape. The window frames were empty of glass. Carefully, I pressed my feet against the seat, wrapped my hands around the outside of the car through the window, and lay sideways facing the sky. I pulled myself through the hole slowly until I was in a sitting position with just my legs left in the car. I finished the job and finally found myself standing on dirt and glass.

I removed the blood stained shirt from my torso and wiped my face, then ripped the left sleeve off. Wrapped around my leg, it would slow the bleeding as I climbed to the road. The climb went by much like the fall did, timeless in a sense, as my mind spun. It would have been an easy climb for me any other day but it wasn't easy now. Every reach towards the heavens struck a thunderbolt of pain throughout my entire body. And then at last, the ledge appeared.

I forced one last, mighty push against the soil and managed to throw my body to the top of the ridge and pull myself up. In the distance – perhaps 300 yards - my eyes now beheld a small red farmhouse. Without any further thought, I began to sprint towards it, pushing aside all connection to the throbbing pain I was experiencing. But no sooner than 25 feet did my injury triumph over me and I collapsed to the ground. I could feel the moisture on my irritated leg from the drenched and dripping cloth around it. Running was out of the question. I began my strides again, slower and shorter.

Walking to the house seemed an endless distance. At last I reached the freshly painted white front door and began pounding and screaming for help. I collapsed again. The door suddenly opened wide and a man around my father's age was looking down at me.

"Please… help…, please… help me!"

I blurted out.

"My… family… is—"

The words spilled out incoherently. The man dropped to his knees and pulled me up into a sitting position. He put both of his hands on my sweaty, bloody face, held it firmly and tried to quiet my hysteria.

"Calm down, son," he said. "I'll help you but I have to know what it is you're trying to tell me."

"My family... my family, my baby sister is..."

Try as I might to force the words into something he would understand, the best I could do was to choke and wildly flail my arms in the direction of the accident.

"All right, son," he said calmly. "Why don't you just go and show me?"

I grabbed his hand, fervently wishing that I wasn't too late, that this stranger would somehow know exactly what to do and that my family would be rescued as a result.

At the edge of the road, he tried to convince me to stay where I was. Through hot tears, I adamantly refused. "We can save them," I remember insisting.

By the time we reached the site we discovered that we weren't alone. People I had never seen before had already gotten out of their cars and were gawking at the wreckage. "Looks pretty bad," I heard two young women remark, pointing to several young men who were in the process of removing three lifeless bodies from the car.

"No!" I screamed, running towards them. "My family! My sister!"

I felt a strong pair of arms grab me. It was the farmer, trying as hard he could to shield me from so unforgettable a sight as death. I fought him as best as I knew how but, in the end, exhaustion overcame me. I was put in one of the cars on the side of the road.

"Please Lord," I begged, "just give me my family back." My mind raced over every possible transgression I had ever made that would warrant so awful a fate. "I don't have anyone else," I implored. "You can't do this to me. Please, Lord, don't do this. I promise that I'll never sin again."

I remember making a quick glance towards Gina's body in the near expectation of movement.

The thought of never again hearing her laughter or seeing the warmth of her eyes turned me cold. How could a merciful god inflict such pain?!

I watched through glassy eyes as a pair of ambulances appeared a short while later. They took me to the nearest hospital and the bodies of my family – sheets drawn over their faces - were put in the second emergency vehicle. Two doctors awaited our arrival in the ER. They first stitched up the laceration on my right leg and then tended to my face, examining each cut and scratch, pulling out any slivers of glass that remained. The doctors reassured me there would be little to no scarring on my skin. Scarring. How could any scars on the outside of my body ever hope to match the pain that burned within?

An hour later, I found myself in radiology for x-rays. "Discoloration and frailty," I overheard someone say. "Poor thing." I had no internal injuries, they told me, but was to stay overnight in the infirmary.

Covered in bulky white blankets on a thin

hospital mattress, I shivered the whole night through, unable to shake the fragile image of Gina on the backseat of the car. The scent of bloodstained leather filled my nostrils. Again and again, I replayed the sight of my parents' mangled bodies. I heard glass crunching and metal crumpling as our car smashed against the rocks. This will never end, I thought. Never, as long as I live.

And then I watched the sun slowly rise.

* * *

Mrs. Scarpetti was a widow in her early 50's who lived next door to us and who had become somewhat of a surrogate grandmother to Gina and me. "Why doesn't she have any children of her own?" I remember asking Mama when I was young. Mama didn't know. Nor did she seem to know how Mrs. Scarpetti's husband had died, only that Mrs. Scarpetti would sometimes talk about him as if he had just gone to the store and would return at any moment.

Mrs. Scarpetti also liked to garden and had an abundance of flowers and vegetables to show for her efforts. "She has a green thumb," my father said. When I was little, this was a source of great curiosity to me, especially since both of her thumbs looked exactly like everyone else's. I remember, too, that she seemed to have only one outfit, a shapeless cotton dress that she alternately accessorized with a sweater and an apron.

It, therefore, surprised me to see her in something so different from her usual ensemble when she came to the hospital and signed the papers for my release. "I am taking you home, Corrado," she said quietly.

She was wearing a black wool dress - a choice that seemed strange to me given the warmth of the weather – and she had traded her customary sandals for a pair of sturdy black shoes with squared toes. Only the slender silver crucifix that dangled from a chain around her neck had made the transition to her radical change of wardrobe.

I also noticed she had brought a small paper bag which she set at the foot of my bed. With an apologetic smile she told me that she had guessed at the size and hoped it was right. "You've grown so fast lately, I wasn't sure," she added. And with that, she discreetly stepped out of the room, leaving me to change into the plain cotton shirt and pair of pants that the bag contained.

I would have preferred my own clothes but they were nowhere in sight. Angered that they had been taken away without asking, I proceeded to pull on a top that felt too small and pants that felt too big. Still, I could not fault Mrs. Scarpetti's kindness in buying me something new with her own money.

A taxicab was waiting for us just outside the entrance. An extravagance, I thought, and one that struck me as well beyond Mrs. Scarpetti's modest pension. Still, I was too tired to ask questions and simply marveled at how large the backseat was compared to—

I felt the sting of tears start to come to my eyes but I didn't want Mrs. Scarpetti to see. She might think it was because I didn't like the clothes or that I wasn't being the "brave little man" the nurses had kept calling me.

She didn't say more than a few words to me

during the ride. But it wasn't conversation I needed…
or wanted. Her silent presence was comfort enough
for me at the moment and, before I knew it, I had
fallen asleep.

* * *

The sound of the engine shutting off brought me groggily awake and I realized that the taxicab had pulled to a stop in front of our house. I reached for the door handle to let myself out but Mrs. Scarpetti's hand firmly gripped my wrist before I could make my exit. "I need you to stay right here," she said.

Puzzled, I watched her climb out of the vehicle and start down the path towards the front door. Why hadn't she wanted me to go with her, I wondered. She let herself in with the key my parents always kept in their secret place. I fidgeted restlessly as I waited for her to come out, trying to grasp a plausible explanation of what was going on. The taxicab driver seemed to sense my disquiet and tried to engage me in conversation. I smiled politely and turned my attention back to the window.

I blinked my eyes in happy amazement at

what I saw. Gina was playing in the front yard with her dolls. Mama was visible through the kitchen window fixing supper before Papa came home from work. "Did you say something?" the driver asked, responding to my joyous – and obviously audible - gasp of astonishment.

"It's my family!" I exclaimed. As I excitedly pointed my finger toward the house, the image vanished as quickly as it came, replaced by the sight of Mrs. Scarpetti now carrying a large cardboard box as she stepped out into the sunlight. Gentleman that he was, the driver hurriedly got out to assist her.

By the time she got into the backseat for the remaining short drive to her house next door, rivulets of hot tears were streaming down my face and my body was convulsing. Mrs. Scarpetti protectively put her arm around me, murmuring to me in our native language that everything was going to be all right. I gulped hard, trying to smother the sobs but to no avail. "They were <u>here</u>," I said. "I <u>saw</u> them."

Whether or not she believed me, I wasn't sure.

* * *

Evidence of Mrs. Scarpetti's devout Catholicism could not be overlooked in the tidy dwelling she called home. Religious paintings, a thick Bible, and an ornamental cross in prominent display in her dining room reminded me that Sundays were the only time I never saw her out working in her garden. A green and white embroidered pillow occupied an armchair where Mrs. Scarpetti liked to do her reading of the newspaper. The words on it were Irish, I remembered, and meant to comfort those whose lives were undergoing turmoil:

God - grant me the serenity to accept the things
I cannot change;
courage to change the things I can;
and wisdom to know the difference.

There were pictures of her husband, too, many of them standing next to Mrs. Scarpetti when she was much younger than she was now and when she wore her hair down to her waist instead of pinned into a tight bun.

The aroma of leftover Easter ham permeated the small kitchen as she started to prepare our lunch. Mrs. Scarpetti, without question, was a very good cook. But then, so was Mama.

She glanced over and caught me looking at what she had put into the box. Most of it was just clothing – my own – along with some loose pictures and a few books she thought I'd like to have. "In a few days, I can go get back and get some more," she said.

I listened to her with growing bewilderment, my expectation being that sometime after lunch I'd walk back next door, sleep in my own bed, and try to figure out what was going to happen next. Vague and shadowy as the future looked, I needed to surround myself with things that were familiar and that reminded me of the family I had lost.

After a moment, she wiped her hands on the front of her apron and pulled out the chair closest to me. "It has been decided," she gently began, "that you will be living here…with me…from now on."

I only half-listened, as angered at whomever had made such a decision on my behalf as I was at whomever had stolen my clothes at the hospital.

"God has given me – and us - this opportunity," she was explaining. "I know that what I'm going to tell you… a lot of it you won't be able to understand." She reached out and pushed an unruly lock of hair off my forehead. "You must have faith, Corrado. It is what He wants of us."

I looked down, trying to focus on the intricate pattern of the lacey white tablecloth.

"Everything will be all right," she reassured me. "I have lots of room here and we can buy whatever you need that will make you comfortable.

I can send you to school as well, and when the day comes that you decide what you want to be —"

Her words trailed off. I looked up and she was earnestly searching my face for a sign that I understood what she was trying to tell me.

"Thank you for the clothes," I murmured, realizing I had forgotten to say something earlier in acknowledgment of her gift.

Her leathery face broke into a grin as she leaned forward to hug me. "Oh, Corrado! It is I who should be thanking you for coming into my life!" Her cheerful segue to reminiscence about when she first met me and, later, when my little sister was born was discomfiting to me in light of what had happened only the day before.

My eyes met hers and something in the way I looked at her made her stop talking altogether. How long we sat there, I'm not sure. It was Mrs. Scarpetti who finally broke the awkward silence. "I understand the pain you are feeling," she said. "I know because

I have felt the same pain of loss myself." She shook her head sadly. "You will never be able to forget what happened…not for as long as you live. You will never be able to forget the feelings, the sights, the smells of that day…"

I squirmed in my chair, wishing that I were anywhere but in this room and hearing anything but the grim prediction that no amount of time would ever make me whole.

Reluctantly, she continued what she was saying. "When my husband died, many friends offered me condolence with the words, 'time will heal your pain.' Franco left me 23 years ago and not a day has passed I haven't missed his company. I still find myself alone in bed late at night with tears and wishing that…" She broke off, perhaps embarrassed to be confiding her sorrow to someone so young.

I swallowed hard, trying not to show my anger that she could bring up her own ancient loss of one beloved to my most recent loss of three. Didn't she understand? I had no one. I had no mother or father. I had no home, no family. And she wanted to compare our losses?

"There is not a single day," she went on, "that I doubt his presence and his watching over me. Let me help you, Corrado. Let me care for you. I cannot take the sadness from your heart, but I can give you a good home."

She waited for me to reply but I had returned my focus to the lace tablecloth. As if from a distance, I heard her push back the chair and stand up. "The decision rests with you," she said. "Should you not wish to stay with me, then tell me and I will understand."

A cold knot had formed in my stomach. How could I reject the kindness of her offer when, in truth, I had nowhere else to go?

"I can stay," I said.

A smile of relief spread across Mrs. Scarpetti's face.

"Good," she replied. "Now let's see about some lunch…"

* * *

The days under Mrs. Scarpetti's roof soon stretched into months without my realizing it. Every morning I would wake to a full breakfast on the table, and would sleep on fresh linen every night. I helped around the house as much as I could and never once complained. Maybe it was my imagination but my own thumbs even began to turn green after the amount of time I spent digging in the garden with my benefactor.

Mrs. Scarpetti had certainly stuck to her word; she had made me a home. Having a home, though, wasn't the same as having a family. I was reminded of that every time I stepped outside and looked next door. My family's things had long since been moved out. Mrs. Scarpetti had judiciously separated the items that had personal and nostalgic value from those that could be given away or sold.

For the latter, she had purchased a small ledger book and dutifully recorded every sale, promising me that the money would be put in an account at the bank on my behalf.

No amount of money in the world, though, would ever bring back Mama, Papa and Gina.

"Do you have any family?" I asked Mrs. Scarpetti one night as we washed the dishes. She never spoke of any and I was curious.

"I have you," she replied without hesitation.

"Besides me."

She considered my question for a moment. "A brother in Spain who's much older," she said, "but disagreeable enough to have driven everyone off." She added with a trace of humor in her voice that three of those who fled in exasperation had been his own wives. There was a niece and two nephews, too, she went on, but they had long since relocated to America and rarely even wrote letters to her.

An idea suddenly jumped into my head,

nearly causing me to drop the plate I was drying.

"What is it?" she wanted to know, startled by my new-found euphoria and undisguised in her anxiety about the jeopardy it might bring to her heirloom china.

"I have an uncle!" I blurted out. "My Uncle Alfredo! He lives in America!" How I had put him out of my memory up until now was a mystery to me but the mere mention of his name magically represented a golden ticket I might never have imagined for myself.

"Slow down!" Mrs. Scarpetti insisted, unable to keep up with my rapid tumble of words. "Take it from the beginning…"

I took a deep breath and began to recount how my uncle, Alfredo Gordini, had left Sicily in the winter of 1946. He had a beautiful new bride and big dreams. Unfortunately, he also had no money, a problem all too common among men who sought to leave a significant mark on the world. Mrs. Scarpetti smiled sympathetically at his plight and urged me to continue my story.

Because Lessante had few opportunities for employment, I explained, Uncle Alfredo realized that the only way he could make a good home for his wife - and the many children he knew they would have – was to go to New York. "He'd find a job," I said, "and save enough money for his wife to join him."

The passage of a year, however, failed to bring him the dream he so cherished. It also brought him a heartache he had never anticipated. "People like to gossip," I said, embarrassed that my own father was not above guilt in that particular regard. When he learned that his sister-in-law had not only fallen in love with another man but was also carrying his child – I felt myself blush at this sinful disclosure - Papa felt it was incumbent upon him to let Alfredo know what was going on. The latter was devastated.

He had been living at the time in a dump

of a loft in Brooklyn. "When he got Papa's letter," I went on, "he moved out of the Italian community immediately."

Mrs. Scarpetti thoughtfully nodded, affirming that there was no greater shame an Italian husband could endure.

"Papa never heard from him again," I said. "He'd talk to Gina and me about him, though." In my mind's eye, I always saw my uncle as someone courageous and fearless who was forging a name for himself in an unknown land. I had never told anyone before now but I pictured him like a valiant hero from the pages of my books.

"He sounds very brave," Mrs. Scarpetti remarked. "Very brave…and very much alone."

"He won't be alone much longer!" I announced.

She tilted her head in puzzlement.

"I'm going to America to find him," I informed her. "He's not going to be alone anymore."

Her look was one of faint amusement at my youthful display of bravado. It would not be until many years later that I would think back on that evening and recognize her response for what it was – a brave mask to hide the pain of realizing my uncle's state of abandonment and loneliness would very soon be traded for her own.

* * *

It's one thing to announce that one is going to America. It's quite another to actually get there. Mrs. Scarpetti reminded me that my age – and the lack of a visa – were obstacles that could not be taken lightly. "How are you going to get there?" Mrs. Scarpetti asked me. "The transportation is not cheap."

"I'll think of something," I confidently replied, though the truth was that I had no idea where to begin.

"And what about your uncle?" she pressed. "Do you know where he lives?"

I told her that I didn't think he'd be very hard to find. Since he had gone to America to make an important name for himself, surely whomever I asked would have heard of him.

Mrs. Scarpetti did not seem to share my

optimism. "New York is a big place," she said. "Without an address to go on—"

"I'll find him," I insisted. It wasn't just that I <u>wanted</u> to. I <u>had</u> to. He was all the family I had left.

"You will always have me, Corrado," she said.

In my heart, I knew that. Still, it wasn't the same.

During the week that followed, I continued to talk about my plans. Mrs. Scarpetti would listen for a few minutes and then casually change the subject to something else. Couldn't she see how determined I was? Like my father, I knew there was an answer to every problem as long as you just looked hard enough to find it.

Impatient to wait any longer, I approached her on Saturday morning as she was outside on both knees and industriously digging in the garden.

"I'm going to America tomorrow," I announced.

Mrs. Scarpetti sighed. "Just look at our poor tomatoes," she said. "They look a little sad now but just you wait. In no time at all we'll have some juicy red ones for our kitchen."

I cleared my throat, wondering whether or not she had heard me. "I'll be leaving tomorrow," I said. "For America."

She paused for a long moment, slowly pulling off one of her gardening gloves and then the other. Without looking up, she quietly reminded me that the next day was Sunday.

"Yes," I said. "It's a good day for traveling, don't you think?"

"Not on Sunday," she said. "You know that, Corrado."

I knew that Sundays were sacred to her. I also knew that she had never forced me to go to church with her, happy as I think it might have made her. My plan, in fact, was that Sunday seemed a perfect time for my departure because she was going to be busy all day and, therefore, wouldn't have the time to miss me.

My words began to flow faster. "I was thinking I don't need that much money to get to Genoa," I explained. I remembered Genoa only briefly from a train trip we'd taken two summers before. "It won't be that hard. I've been there before, you see, and so I know just where to get off, and then all I have to do is—"

I don't know at what point she had stopped listening to me. I could tell she wasn't listening because she was looking off into space the way she'd sometimes get when she talked about her husband.

I touched her shoulder. "Mrs. Scarpetti?"

"Yes?" she answered in a voice that sounded far away and tiny.

"I want to do this," I said. "I want to find my uncle in New York."

"And what then?" she asked.

"What?"

She finally looked at me and I saw that her eyes were moist with tears. "This uncle of yours," she said, "do you know for certain that he'll take you in and let you live with him?"

I was momentarily speechless that such a thought would even cross her mind. "He's my uncle," I said. "He <u>has</u> to."

She gently reminded me that he was someone I had never met and who may, in fact, have obligations that didn't include a 15 year old boy.

I was determined to prove her wrong. "I'll send you a picture of us together," I vowed. "Then you'll see how that it all worked out."

"I hope so, Corrado," she replied. "For your sake, I truly hope so."

I brightened. "Does that mean I can go then?"

My entire fate now hung on the brittle silence that hovered between us.

"Yes," she said at last. "But not until Monday."

* * *

"Are you sure you don't want me to go with you to Genoa?" she asked as we ate dinner together on Sunday evening.

A part of me wanted to invite her along to keep me company on the train. Another part of me, though, wondered in suspicion whether she'd use the duration of the ride to try to talk me out of leaving. "I'll be fine," I assured her, suddenly feeling very grown up and worldly. I could see that she was starting to feel sad again and so I told her that I'd heard there were lots of trains in New York and that I'd probably be riding them quite a lot once I settled in at my uncle's house. "And you can come and visit," I said, already feeling as if I knew my way around New York even though I'd never set foot in it.

"You'll need to get there first," she reminded me. "Are you sure you have enough money?"

To my surprise, she had given me a small leather pocketbook containing half the proceeds from the sale of my family's belongings. The other half, she told me, would remain safely in the account she had set up for me at the bank. I knew I probably could have asked for the whole thing but I realized it was her way of extracting an unspoken promise I'd come back for it someday.

She also gave me my mother's wedding ring. "Maybe you'll meet a nice girl when you're older and want her to have it," she told me. That night before I went to bed, I slipped it onto a chain so I could wear it around my neck and keep it tucked out of sight under my shirt. I also folded the equivalent of $10 in lira and stuffed it into the toe of one shoe, mindful of Mrs. Scarpetti's warning not to carry all of my money in one place.

Despite my insistence that I knew what I was doing, she was understandably nervous insofar as how I was going to get on board a ship if I didn't have papers. "People do it all the time," I assured her, even though I personally didn't know of any who had been successful. The trick, I said, was just to make friends with someone who worked at the docks and to give them some money to sneak you aboard. Money, I had figured out at a young age, seemed to be a universal language that everyone from the highest to the lowest could understand. Mrs. Scarpetti was dubious about my improvised strategy and cautioned me not to let anyone know I had anything more than the lira in my shoe.

I lay in bed that night with my eyes wide open, too excited about my upcoming journey to let sleep overtake me. Worried thoughts began to creep into my mind. Would I be able to find him? Would he accept me into his house? What if he isn't even alive anymore? What if I didn't make it to New York alive?

My hand went to my chest and my fingers closed around the ring. I missed Mama.

Whenever I had trouble sleeping, she would sit right next to my bedside, run her fingers through my hair and softly sing me to sleep.

"Hmmm… hmmm…" I quietly hummed the tune to myself, and the room became darker and darker.

The train for Genoa was leaving at 6 a.m. Mrs. Scarpetti had called for a taxicab to take us to the station where she would see me off. Neither of us knew what to say to one another, sobered by the realization that, from this day forward, nothing would be the same.

She waited with me until my train arrived. And when it did, there were still no words to describe what we were feeling. Both of us held back tears at a final embrace.

I picked up the single piece of luggage I had and walked to the train. Once I entered it, I walked all the way to the back of the car and sat in a window seat, my suitcase at my feet. I could see Mrs. Scarpetti sitting in the same spot, with her hands in her lap and her purse on her arm.

"All aboard!"

I heard the conductor shout. I let out a deep breath.

"Last call!"

My eyes were locked on Mrs. Scarpetti as the locomotive began to move. With what looked like a heavy sigh of resignation, she got to her feet. I didn't want to watch her fade away and so I shut my eyes tight and began to softly hum to myself until I fell asleep.

Some time later I awoke to the sound of a baby crying. My eyes quickly darted to my feet. My suitcase was still there. I looked to my left where a lady now occupied the neighboring seat with her fussy infant daughter.

"Sshhh, it's okay baby, ssshhhhh."

The woman gently rocked back and forth. Her voice was so soothing and calm that it instantly put me at ease.

The baby's fussing finally came to an end. The little girl was looking right at me with the biggest brown eyes I'd ever seen. They were almost as pretty as Gina's. With a gurgled laugh, she reached towards my arm. I put up my hand to give her a finger to grasp.

"She's not bothering you, is she?" the lady asked in concern.

"No, not at all," I replied, torn between confiding that I'd had a baby sister who looked just like her and, at the same time, knowing such disclosure would only bring a lump to my throat.

The woman smiled warmly at me. She was really very pretty, with dark brown hair and freckles on her nose. She seemed young, too, and totally devoted to her child.

The baby eventually lost interest in my hand and rested her head on her mother's shoulder for a nap. I leaned the other way, my head against a cold window, and tried to get some sleep as well to make up for my previous night of restlessness.

I dreamed of everything. I dreamed of my

family and the happy days when we had all been together. I dreamed of the fun I was going to have in New York with my uncle. I dreamed of Mrs. Scarpetti, alone in her home with no one to talk to.

By the time I opened my eyes again, the scenery outside the window was no longer familiar. The seat to the left of me was also empty.

I waved down an older man who was wearing the uniform of a train attendant. "How long until we reach Genoa?" I asked him. To my astonishment, he informed me that we were less than an hour away from the station. I couldn't believe my ears! How could I have slept so soundly for so many hours and not been awakened by the noises and whistles and shuffling of passengers each time we pulled into a different stop along the way?

"Thank you, "I said but the man didn't move on as I had expected him to do. Instead, he was looking at me sternly.

"Riding alone, son?" he inquired.

Unsure of his intentions, I chose my words carefully. "My father's in another car talking to friends," I lied, hoping it sounded casual "He's going to be back any moment."

The man nodded, apparently accepting my reply as a truthful one. "If you need anything before he gets back," he said, "just let me know."

I watched as he made his way down the aisle and disappeared into the next car, relieved on the one hand that he had not stayed to meet him and yet, on the other, not entirely convinced he wouldn't come back later to check. In the event I might need them, my mind was already racing to fashion clever excuses on what might detain my fictitious traveling companion.

I tried to distract myself by eavesdropping on the nearest conversations. I tried counting the number of trees I saw. I even took my shoes off and tried opening and closing the latches of my suitcase with my toes.

And then, before I knew it, I heard the words I'd been waiting for.

We were pulling into the Genoa station.

Corrado "Charlie" Ammatuna

Carlo & Charlie Ammatuna

Charlie with son Louis and daughter Anmarie

Rosa, Charlie & Carlo Ammatuna

* * *

It was even bigger and busier than I remembered from those two summers before. As I grabbed my suitcase and started to disembark, I saw the same man again and a ripple of apprehension coursed through my body. If he didn't see me leave the train with my "father", would he assume I was a runaway and call the police? I dreaded to imagine what might happen if I were caught. Would they send me back to Lessante…or somewhere else?

I quickly fell in step with a tall man who was struggling at that moment with one of his wife's hatboxes. "Let me help you, sir," I gallantly offered, flashing my most charming smile.

"What a sweet young man," the lady remarked, encouraging her husband to give me the box. Happily, I took it with my free hand and accompanied them to the platform, chatting amiably the whole time about what a beautiful day it was. I didn't look back but I was confident the man had been convinced by my ruse and lost any further interest in me.

The woman thanked me again when we emerged from the station. "You should give him something for his trouble, Peter," she urged her husband. Somewhat grudgingly, he reached into his coat pocket and withdrew a couple of coins. I grinned. That I hadn't been in Genoa for more than five minutes and had already earned money was a sign that seemed to bode well for the rest of the trip.

I inhaled a deep breath of Genoa air and took stock of my bearings. Total strangers smiled at me, just as they had smiled at Papa and me whenever we took trips together to the city. I knew that I echoed his every mannerism from his long stride to the quizzical way he'd pause in front of shop windows and make up funny stories about the kind of people who might wear the clothes and shoes that were on display.

Fashion – especially women's fashion – made little sense to him most of the time and he was not shy about criticizing much of what he saw.

I glanced around in all directions, unsure of what to do next. It had been easy to be confident when I was with Papa because Papa always knew where he was going. I reminded myself that I knew where I was going, too – America. All I had to do was figure out how to get across the ocean that currently divided us.

The station sat on the highest point in the city, where you could see the harbor perfectly. I stood there for a moment at the top of the hill, gazing down at the sea. I began to count the ships along the waterfront but soon got lost in the colors and chaos. I had never seen anything like this before - such an intricate, friendly and delicate structure of so many ships and yet, at the same time, there was something big, bold and intimidating about it. I finally started down the hill towards the docks. People of all kinds roamed the streets and sidewalks, all of them walking with a level of confidence that suggested they had lived there all their lives.

I saw a family standing on the corner just ahead of me. The mother had hold of a young son in each hand. Twins, perhaps. I wasn't sure.

"Excuse me," I began. "Excuse me, sir? Ma'm? I'm looking for the ship going to America. Can you help me?"

The two little boys stared at me.

"Don't stare!" their mother snapped at them.

I repeated my question but the man simply looked past me as if I were invisible. Beneath his breath as I walked away, I heard him mutter the word "beggar" to his wife.

Beggar indeed!

Confused but not defeated, I decided I might have better luck if I sat outside a bar closer to the docks. Sailors and sea captains liked to pass their time in such places, I remembered Papa saying.

Maybe someone on a crew would come out drunk and, mistaking me for one of their own, walk me aboard a ship as easily as I had just walked off the train with a pair of total strangers.

I parked myself on a bench outside the first bar I found and wondered how long it would take for good luck to find me.

I allowed my gaze to wander for a bit. A small group of girls were standing on the corner closest to me and laughing. Who were they waiting for? Maybe they were all college girls, waiting for their house leader to return and lead them out of this part of town. On second thought, though, they didn't look classy enough to be college girls. Tourists, maybe, waiting on a tour guide? They all wore narrow skirts to their knees and blouses that could not have clung to their bodies more if they had been soaking wet. They also wore more make-up than I had seen on clowns at the circus.

One girl stood out. She seemed bored,

almost, and not nearly as anxious as her friends. She was actually rather pretty; prettier than the rest. She caught me glancing over so I quickly averted my eyes. I casually turned my head to the corner across the street, as if I was looking for something. Much to my surprise, there was a similar group of girls gathered on that corner, too, watching and waiting just like the ones nearest me.

It finally occurred to me what these girls were waiting for. They were "Ladies of the Night" as Papa called them. I looked back at the group closest to me to see if the pretty girl had stopped paying attention to my presence. Instead, she was staring right at me. I looked away again but, from the corner of my eye, I saw that she was now approaching me. My legs went numb. I tried to think of what to do. Should I get up? She might think I was interested in her services if I did that. I couldn't stay seated, though. She might try to talk to me, and then what would I say? By the time I decided I should get up and start walking in the other direction it was too late.

"Hey there," she said. She reeked of perfume. "My name's Helena. What's yours?"

The blood began to pound in my temples. Should I tell her my name? My real name? Would she want to know what I was doing there?

She smiled. "Cat got your tongue, honey?"

"Uh….Corrado."

"Corrado," she echoed, licking her red lips as if savoring the sound.

"Yes," I said. "Corrado."

She made no pretense of looking me over. "Little young to be here, aren't you?"

I opened my mouth to respond but realized I had no words to give back in reply.

"That's okay," she said. "I can tell this is your first time." She sat down on the bench next to me. "I noticed you staring at me."

I should have moved away or stood up but I was too paralyzed with confusion to move.

"So you want to go somewhere?" she was now asking.

"No," I blurted out in panic, embarrassed that my voice suddenly had a definitive squeak to it. "I meant I'm not interested in you," I hastily tried to explain. "You're pretty and everything but it's just that I'm not—uh—I mean I don't want—uh—" I was desperately scrambling for the right words to make her go away and leave me alone. "I'm – uh – waiting for a man to come out of the bar." The moment the words left my mouth, I realized by her facial expression I had just made it far worse. My breath quickened and my cheeks became warm as I tried to tell her that I hadn't meant it to sound like I was a—

Was she laughing at me? I wasn't sure. "Thank goodness," she said. "That would be such a waste…"

I had no idea what she was talking about but assumed she was going to get up now and rejoin her friends. Instead she asked me what I was really doing there.

I wasn't sure if I could trust her. Then again, she seemed genuinely interested in my answer. I also suspected she knew a lot about sailors and ships.

I took a deep breath and plunged ahead with my story. "I need to get to America and I need someone to help me—"

She put both hands up as if in mock surrender. "I'm not a babysitter, honey," she curtly informed me. "I'm a working woman. If you want to get yourself to America, it's not going to be on <u>my</u> money."

"<u>I</u> have money," I boasted, a little too loudly. Two of her friends looked over at us. I lowered my voice. "I just need someone to get me on a ship to New York."

Helena folded her arms. "If you've got money, why don't you just buy a ticket?"

"Not <u>that</u> much money," I said. If she made me prove it, I'd take off my shoe and pretend that the lira was all I had to my name. That and the coins in my pocket.

"What are you going to do if you don't get there?" she asked. "Go back home?"

The swell of pain I felt was beyond tears as I replied. "I don't <u>have</u> a home," I whispered. "Not anymore."

I don't know what it was that touched a raw chord of emotion with her. I knew it was unmanly but my emotions got the better of me and I buried my head in my hands. Then again, maybe she just felt embarrassed to be sitting on a bench outside a bar with a teenager who couldn't stop sobbing. "Listen," she said, "a kid like you can't stick around here or you'll get into trouble." She put her hand on my knee and I didn't try to move away. "I've got a flat a couple streets away. You can stay the night. Just <u>one</u> night," she emphasized. "We'll figure out something tomorrow."

Her sudden change of heart was baffling to

me but I was too exhausted – even after all the sleep I'd had – to turn down her offer.

"Give me your hand," she instructed.

I took my right hand from my pocket and opened my sweaty palm. Helena pulled a pen from the purple purse draped over her arm and began to scribble numbers and words on my skin. "Now I've gotta work. I'll see you later tonight." She stood, adjusted her skirt, then turned and strolled back to her corner.

"No luck?" I heard one of her companions ask. Helena's response was a shrug of indifference.

I looked down at my hand. *23 Norte Street*. I had no idea which direction it was but I did know one thing; it was one step closer to America.

* * *

The Spartan flat reeked of the same perfume as Helena. What would Mrs. Scarpetti think of my circumstances, I wondered. I closed my eyes and tried to picture what she would be doing as the day edged toward darkness. Was she alone at the dining room table and having her dinner? Was she sitting in the armchair and reading her Bible? Was she thinking of me? I looked at my immediate surroundings and saw no evidence of warmth, security…or family. Was Helena alone in the world, too, I mused. Had her parents been taken from her as mine had been taken from me? Or had she been the one to leave them and never go back? I tried to imagine what they might think of this disturbing life she had chosen for herself. Unbidden, a new thought came to me. Had Helena once made an ambitious plan to go somewhere else – maybe even America – but given up hope? I shuddered at this prospect, wondering how I'd survive if Genoa was as far as I was going to get.

A little past ten, Helena returned to the flat. To the scent of perfume had now been added the aroma of cigarettes. "Want some coffee?" she said, a little surprised, I think, that I had waited up for her.

"Uh-huh," I answered, not entirely sure of what was going to happen next.

"Want to tell me the rest?" she asked a few minutes later as we sat across from each other at her wobbly dinette table.

"The rest?"

"Your family. What happened to them?"

It was well after midnight by the time I finished. "I'm sorry, Corrado," she murmured. I thought she was going to touch my hand but instead she only reached for another cigarette.

I was determined to resume my journey in the morning, I told her. "Once I find my uncle—"

"How do you know he'll even <u>want</u> you?" she bluntly interrupted.

"You sound like Mrs. Scarpetti," I said.

"And she sounds very wise," Helena pointed out. "Just because we want something more than anything doesn't mean that someone else is going to feel exactly the same."

I wasn't sure if she was talking about my situation or her own but I wisely chose not to pursue it. "So can you help me or not?" I wanted to know.

The cigarette dangled precariously between her lips as she spoke. "If I hadn't picked you up, Corrado, where would you have spent the night?"

I shrugged. "There's a big park. I could have slept under a tree."

She smiled. "You're very enterprising, aren't you?" she observed.

I proudly informed her that I took after my father.

"And I'm sure it's late enough that he'd

want you to be in bed by now," she replied, standing up and grabbing the chipped ceramic ashtray. She paused in the doorway of her tiny kitchen. "You're on the couch," she said.

Before she got out of earshot, I had to ask again whether she was going to help me. If the answer was going to be no, there was no sense for me to stay until morning.

Her lips parted in a seductive smile. "I'll sleep on it," she teased.

* * *

Helena had a friend – a Signore Zotti - she wanted me to meet. Over a hasty breakfast of undercooked eggs and burnt toast, she told me he was a food supplier and had his own agency that dealt with people all over the world. She alluded he had done all right for himself during the war. "He also owes me some big-time favors," she cryptically added.

As I waited for her to get dressed in the next room, I couldn't help but wonder whether her relationship with Signore Zotti had ever been more than platonic. I was pretty sure she wouldn't tell me if I came straight out and asked. It was funny, I reflected, how she had learned my entire life story the previous night and yet I still didn't know the first thing about her. Not even her last name. Maybe it was better not to.

Just as we started to leave, she asked me why I was bringing along my suitcase. "It's not like you'll be boarding a ship by lunch," she said.

How could I bring myself to tell her that I didn't feel safe leaving any part of myself in a flat that someone could just walk into. Certainly I wasn't the only person to whom she had confided where she kept the spare key. "I should have it just in case," I replied.

"Suit yourself," she said.

We took a city bus to an industrial area that Mrs. Scarpetti might have labeled as "unsavory". A few blocks from where it dropped us off was what looked like a warehouse.

"Is this where he lives?" I asked.

Helena corrected me. "It's where he spends his time."

We entered an office on the ground floor and she told me to wait in the reception area. "Signore Zotti is expecting me," she informed the woman behind the desk.

I didn't remember Helena making a phone call from her flat to tell him she was coming but, a few moments later, an interior door opened and there he was - a husky man in his mid-40s with a sharp nose, high cheekbones and dressed to impress, as they say. His hair was slightly gray and thinning but his demeanor was such that he looked like a man one wouldn't want to cross. He greeted Helena with a kiss. "And what can I do for you?" he inquired. Though he didn't outwardly acknowledge my presence, I had a feeling his dark eyes never missed a thing.

"I have a favor to ask of you," she replied, tilting her head slightly in my direction.

I expected him to invite us into his office but apparently he deemed whatever favor she was about to ask would take no more than a minute.

"My friend Corrado needs to go to America and as soon as possible," she said.

He arched an amused brow. "And what has

this new 'friend' of yours done that warrants so hasty a departure from Genoa?"

Helena was quick to read the inference behind his question. "He's a good person," she told him. "He wants to be reunited with his family."

Signore Zotti glanced in my direction. A cynical smile came to his lips as he pointed at my suitcase. "I see he's already packed..."

I held my breath, waiting to hear what Helena would say next on my behalf.

"You're really his only chance," she said. "I was thinking that with all of your connections—"

"Why does this fall on me?" he wanted to know. "He seems old enough to fend for himself."

I was tired of them speaking about me as if I were not in the room. I cleared my throat. "I have some money," I said. As he turned to look at me, I realized I had just made a terrible mistake.

He began strolling toward me, stopping just a few feet from where I sat. I wasn't sure whether I should lower my gaze and stare at the floor or look up at him and try to convey courage. I suddenly felt ill-quipped to pursue either option.

He didn't say anything for what seemed like an eternity. "No amount of money," he finally said, "is worth jeopardizing my business." He turned back to address Helena. "You, of all people, should know that by now."

Was she going to scream at him? Was she going to cry? Was she going to plead my case? To my shock, she did none of these things. With a defiant toss of her hair, she slung her purse over her shoulder and walked toward me, holding out her hand in invitation to conclude our business. Unless I was mistaken, Signore Zotti was as surprised as I was.

"That's it?" he challenged her. "You're leaving?"

Helena smiled at him. "We'll find someone else to help us," she said.

Signore Zotti chuckled. "Who?"

My companion nonchalantly shrugged and ignored his question. "I never realized before what a smart businessman you are," she complimented him. "As I see now, this is not profitable for you and, therefore, you're not interested." She leaned forward and gave him a peck on the cheek. "Goodbye, Signore Zotti. I hope that I'll never have a chance to disrupt your business again."

He caught her wrist before she could take a single step away from him. "What is it with you?" he wanted to know. "I have never seen you so concerned about anyone before." He motioned in my direction, but didn't look at me.

She met his stare evenly and replied, "I have my reasons, but you wouldn't understand." She glanced down at the wrist he so firmly held. "Please let go."

"I ask you again, why are you doing this?"

She drew a deep breath before replying. "I know who I am," she said. "I also know <u>what</u> I am and that I've spent years blaming other people for choices and failures that were my own." Her voice suddenly seemed to soften. "This is finally a chance to do something right for someone else that I'm never even going to see again."

I felt as if my breath were cut off completely as I waited for Signore Zotti's reply. When it came, it was prefaced by him releasing his grip on her wrist and tenderly reaching up to caress the side of her face. "Come into my office," he said to her, though it sounded to me more like a question than a command.

The door closed firmly behind them, leaving me in only the company of the dour-faced receptionist who clearly did not approve of Helena's provocative dress or perfume.

Twenty minutes passed, then thirty. A breathless Helena finally emerged with a radiant grin. "Good news, Corrado!" she exclaimed. "Tomorrow will be a very big day for you!"

✳ ✳ ✳

I had a hundred questions I wanted to ask her but she was too absorbed in planning a special send-off meal for me that night. My heart was tugged back to – how long ago was it now? –Mrs. Scarpetti flitting around her kitchen and making me my favorite things for a farewell feast. Two women, both so very different, and yet each looking out for me in their own ways.

"Have another slice of pizza," Helena insisted.

"Don't you want some more?"

She shook her head and took a long drag on her cigarette. "I'm going to have to leave soon."

I asked her when she was going to be back.

"Not til early morning," came her reply. "Time enough to wish you goodbye."

A new thought crossed my mind. If Signore

Zotti had helped me, maybe he wouldn't mind helping Helena, too. "You could go with me," I suggested.

She laughed. "What silly ideas you get sometimes," she chided me as she refilled my glass with cheap red wine.

We didn't talk about it again but in the back of my mind I've always wondered if she was flattered to be asked.

✳ ✳ ✳

She was already dressed when I woke up the next day. "Signore Zotti called," she said, "There's been a change of plans."

A sheer black fright swept through me. Certainly he hadn't changed his mind during the night? Helena laughed off my anxiety. "You're still going," she assured me. "You just need to get ready a little faster."

Not that there was very much I needed to do. What little I owned had stayed packed ever since I boarded the train for Genoa. In all likelihood, it would stay packed on the ship voyage as well.

At 7:30 a scrawny man in his early 40's knocked on Helena's door and introduced himself as Arturo. He was a cook, he said, on the *SS Horizon*. A cook? The thought nearly made me laugh out loud. Every cook I had ever seen had a big pot belly from sampling their own food too much. Maybe, I mused, Arturo's cooking wasn't that good and he avoided the temptation to overindulge.

"I'm here to pick up the boy," he told us, speaking mostly to Helena.

Helena smiled graciously. "Yes, we've been expecting you. Come on, Corrado, I'll walk with you down to the ship and maybe we can—"

"That's not advised," Arturo sharply cut her off.

Helena looked at him in puzzlement.

"We only want to say goodbye…"

"I don't want to attract any attention when I bring him aboard," Arturo explained. "You'll have to say your goodbyes here."

The next few minutes became a blur to me. The night before - while she was out - I had tried to collect my thoughts so that I could say all the right things to thank her for helping me. And yet now, in the doorway, I couldn't remember a single one of them. Instead, I threw my arms around her waist and hugged her. A teary-eyed Helena hugged me back. "I'm going to miss you very much Corrado."

And with that, she let go.

She stood in the doorway, still wiping away tears and waving at us until we reached the corner. We weren't a block away when I told Arturo I had forgotten something and had to go back. A bewildered Helena opened the door. "I just can't get rid of you, can I?" she remarked, although she said it with a smile.

I had already fumbled inside my shirt and was pulling the chain off my neck, the chain that held my mother's ring. "This ring was my mother's." I told her. "It's important to me. I want you to have it…to thank you for everything." I blinked back the tears that threatened to stifle my voice. "Maybe I'll see you again sometime?"

I didn't wait for her to reply. I just spun around and ran back to Arturo, who had watched the whole exchange in silence.

Getting on the ship was easier than I had imagined. There were people all around us but they were too busy minding their own business to pay attention to who was getting on and off. Arturo had a cabin to himself with a sink and a narrow cupboard for his clothes. There was only one bed and he told me that I would have to put my feet by his head and my head by his feet if we were to both fit.

"Be very quiet," he warned me. "Lock the door at all times and don't answer if someone knocks and it's not me." He could lose his job, he explained, if someone were to see me and discover how I had gotten on board without any papers.

I had overheard that the trip to New York would take a week and now felt compelled to ask Arturo what I could do to pass the time if I wasn't supposed to leave the room.

"That's not my problem," he retorted. And with that, he went out the door, not returning until several hours later with some food from the galley.

Even in that short space of time, I felt as if the tiny compartment were closing in on me. The movement of the ship – even before we got underway – was already making me feel off-balance and nauseous. If I threw up, I told myself, Arturo probably wouldn't hesitate to throw me overboard at his first opportunity.

The *SS Horizon*, Arturo told me when we had walked to the docks, was a very old ship, better than 20 years. It had a crew of 43 and was strong and solid on the outside. Its insides, however, were a different story. The engine was old and noisy and prone to breaking down. I asked him why no one had taken the time to repair it properly or, for that matter, just get a new one. Arturo's curt response was that they were too lazy to care.

"What about the captain?" I asked. Weren't captains supposed to take pride in their ships?

As Arturo explained it to me, apparently this

one did but his repeated requests to company officials had fallen on deaf ears.

"She'll be the death of us someday," Arturo predicted.

I could only hope that it didn't happen until long after I was safe on American shores.

* * *

We had only been out to sea for a few hours –
maybe less - but I had already convinced myself this
was the most horrible experience of my life. Would
it be better or worse, I wondered, if I had a window
to look out of? I had expected to be able to watch
the harbor at Genoa get smaller and smaller until it
finally disappeared from sight. A part of me, I think,
also hoped that if I looked really hard I'd be able
to see Helena waving at me. She had worn a bright
red dress that morning and would not have been that
difficult for me to spot, even at a distance.

The bottom of my feet tickled and sent a
vibrating sensation from my toes to the back of
my neck. Was the whole trip going to be like this,
I worried, with the floorboards trembling as if they
were going to fall apart? I tried laying down and
thinking about other things but the bed vibrated, too.

I silently declared I would never get on another ship as long as I lived.

For the first three days, the weather cooperated…or so I was told. I would like to have been able to go up top for fresh air and see things for myself but I was mindful of betraying Arturo. "There's nothing to see," he'd answer whenever I asked him to describe everything that was going on. There hadn't been much sun but, fortunately, there had been no sign of rain, either.

By the fourth day, everything changed. He told me that we were approaching something called the Ships' Cemetery. I thought at first he only meant to scare me, for certainly the label was ominous enough. By evening, though, Mother Nature unleashed her full fury on us. Vicious winds howled and cataclysmic waves repeatedly pounded us. I hugged a pillow to my face to keep from screaming, certain that we were all going to die. I had felt like this only once before in my life and the terror of it returned to my head with a vengeance. If I had but one thought that sustained me through this nightmare at sea, it was that maybe this was the end and I'd at least be reunited with my family.

In the distance, I heard a shout go up for all hands on deck. What was I to do?! If all the men had been called on deck because they were going to abandon the ship to the hunger of the sea, it would mean that they'd be abandoning me to its wrath as well. My mind raced. Arturo knew that I'd obey his orders to stay out of sight. Did it also mean he'd risk everything to come and get me if my life were in danger? Sadly, I didn't know him well enough to make an accurate guess.

The waves seemed to be growing in intensity. No matter how dearly I tried to hang on to something to steady myself, the deep pitch was flinging me from one side of the compartment to the other. I could now hear frantic footsteps and the muffled sound of orders. I couldn't make out the words above the wail of the storm but I knew it couldn't be good. What if Arturo came back for me and it was too late, I thought. What would he do with my body if I died? In my frightened mind's eye, I saw myself being sacrificed to the Atlantic and disappearing forever into its depths.

I heard shouting again. It was the captain ordering the ship to reduce its speed. Please, I prayed. Please, God, get us through this in one piece.

Someone was furiously pounding on the cabin door. It couldn't be someone looking for Arturo, I realized. Arturo would be up on deck with everyone else. Still, I hesitated. The pounding came again and this time I thought I heard a voice go with it. Arturo!

Drenched and disheveled, he nearly fell into the room on top of me when I opened the door. "Are you all right?" he shouted. Before I could reply, he thrust a towel and some hard bread into my hands. He was gone again before I could ask him anything. But at least he had remembered I was on board. For now, it would have to be enough.

He would later tell me that the storm lasted for two full days but that the old ship had proved her mettle. I relate this because I was too sick, bruised and dehydrated to coherently remember much of anything after that first night of hell. Arturo's concern proved to be that of a genuine friend. He even snuck me one of the captain's steaks - lightly seasoned, tender and hot – to help put some weight back on my bones. "I'm staying until you've finished every last bite," he said.

While he was gone during the day, I tried to entertain myself by imagining what circumstances had brought him into the circle of Signore Zotti's friends. I also wondered about Helena. Had Arturo only <u>pretended</u> they'd never met when he came to the door to get me? I couldn't be sure. I only hoped that Helena was doing all right and that maybe someday she'd meet someone who would treat her well and marry her so she'd never have to work again.

I knew we had to be getting closer to America and my spirits began to feel restored. "What are <u>you</u> going to do when we get there?" I asked Arturo.

Arturo's plan, though, was nowhere as grand as mine. He shrugged, explaining that he would do what he had already done many times before; he would take the ship back to Genoa and the cycle of transport would begin all over again. I was aghast that he'd want to live through any more ocean storms after the one we had just barely survived and asked him why. His only response was that he had been through much worse.

To be honest, I half-hoped that maybe he'd want to stay in New York for a few days and help me find my uncle. I expressed this out loud to see his reaction. "Then when you go back," I continued, "you could go tell Signore Zotti that it turned out all right. Maybe Helena, too."

Arturo contemplated this a moment, a half smile on his unshaven face. In retrospect, how naive

I must have sounded to him in my belief that a businessman like Signore Zotti gave me any further thought once I left his sight at the warehouse. "Men like Zotti—" he started to tell me but then left the sentence unfinished. "There's only going forward," he said, a statement that sounded uncharacteristically philosophical coming from a mouth such as his. "If you dwell too much on things in the past you've had to do—" he left this sentence incomplete as well and told me he needed to get back to the galley.

I lay in bed for a long time after he left, trying to make sense of why so many bad things had happened to people who hadn't really done anything bad to deserve it. There was Mrs. Scarpetti's husband dying. There was my Uncle Alfredo's wife leaving him for another man. There was my family being killed in the accident. There was Helena whose past was too painful for her to even talk about. There also lingered a melancholy about Arturo, too, that I had glimpsed only fleetingly during our time together at sea in cramped quarters. But as Arturo told me, there is only going forward.

* * *

The harsh blast of the ship's whistle brought both of us fully awake at 3:15 in the morning. Out in the corridor, men were shouting and running. "Stay here!" Arturo told me. "I'll see what's going on." He burst back into the cabin in what seemed like only seconds later. "The engine's on fire!" he yelled.

It was even worse than that, I quickly learned. The fire was spreading faster than it could be contained and the captain had given orders to abandon ship. I barely had time to pull my shirt on when Arturo grabbed my arm and told me we had to get up on deck. I could now smell the smoke and panicked at the sight of the crew racing past us. How could a ship be on fire, I remember thinking, when it was sitting in the middle of so much water?!

"Almost there," I heard Arturo say. And then I remembered my suitcase. I tried to turn and run back to the cabin but Arturo grabbed me. "This way!" he shouted.

"But everything I have—"

"The only thing you've got is your life!" he yelled, now pushing me ahead of him so that my return was blocked.

I don't know how we ever made it to the deck. Everything was hot and loud and stuffy and moving much too fast for me to even comprehend. If any of the men noticed the presence of an additional passenger they'd never seen before, they were too panic-stricken to bring attention to it. Somehow in the horror of the shared danger we were experiencing, I had managed to become invisible. Crew members were frantically lowering the lifeboats and Arturo roughly shoved me into the first one we came to. I expected him to jump in right behind me but he had run to assist his fellow sailors. I heard someone say that our distress call had been picked up by another ship and that help was on its way. I fervently prayed that it would get there soon and put the fire out. Maybe the damage wasn't as bad as everyone was saying. And as long as the fire didn't spread down to our cabin there was still a chance that my suitcase would survive unscathed.

My optimism, however, was to be short-lived. The ship was now almost half engulfed in bright orange and yellow flames. I looked around for Arturo and was relieved to see him in another one of the boats. I now heard someone shouting for the captain. I looked around me but I didn't see him in any of the trio of lifeboats that were now bobbing their way away from the inferno. I squinted at the ship and could vaguely make out the outline of the fourth boat that hadn't been lowered into the water yet. A moment later, I could make out the figures of two men, one holding the other up and helping him into the last boat. A surge of admiration coursed through my body as I realized that the stronger of the pair was the captain, valiantly staying aboard the ship until the last of his crew had made it to safety.

The only sight more exciting – though I was still terrified beyond description – was the sound of a helicopter that seemed to come from out of nowhere and was now hovering somewhere above us. In all of the confusion, I had forgotten that we weren't that far from New York. Amazingly, the first arrival of help had come from the sky, not from the sea.

Still, our ordeal was far from over. The helicopter circled overhead a few times and then lowered a group of men onto the ship to try to fight the fire. I learned later that they had failed at this strategy, beaten back by the flames until they were forced to withdraw. Regrouping, they tried again, this time repeatedly pumping seawater directly into the vessel for what seemed an eternity.

Their perseverance at last won out and a collective cheer went up amongst those of us who had helplessly witnessed the entire thing from the lifeboats. Maybe, I thought, God had been watching, too, and decided we needed a little luck to bring us home.

* * *

Dry land at last! Technically, of course, it was only the dry deck of the Coast Guard ship that came to rescue us but the unabashed elation of the crew as they scrambled aboard was a festive sight to behold. Arturo even hugged me, then pretended that he hadn't really meant to.

I drank in a deep breath of fresh air as I huddled in the warmth of a scratchy blanket someone had handed me and that I had wrapped around my body. My shoes were soaked through but I didn't care. Pretty soon I'd be setting foot on the American shores of New York. My ankles, I fancied, may as well have had wings as I caught my first sight of the Statue of Liberty. I had seen pictures in books of the famous lady with the torch but none had done her justice. "Welcome, Corrado Gordini!" she seemed to say. I lifted my right arm as if to return the salute, unaware that this spontaneous and dramatic gesture caught the eye of the last person in the world I wanted to have notice me.

"Who the hell are you?" a stern voice behind me wanted to know.

I froze. It was the captain.

"Answer me!" he ordered. "You're not a stowaway, are you?"

I panicked. If I said no, he'd want to see my papers. Papers that I didn't have. If I told him the truth and said yes – well, I didn't even want to fathom what he was going to do to me.

Other members of the crew were now looking at both of us as the captain jabbed an angry finger at my chest. "How did you get on my ship? Who helped you?"

I swallowed hard, desperately trying to think of a quick story that would save my skin and, more importantly, save my friend Arturo.

The captain repeated his questions, this time

even louder. Maybe I could tell him that my papers had been washed overboard in the storm. Or maybe that they had burned in the fire and that—

The next voice I heard was Arturo's. "It's my fault, sir," he confessed. "I accept full responsibility for the boy."

I couldn't believe my ears. Hadn't he told me time and again that bad things would happen to him if anyone found out what he had done and yet now he was saying it out loud for the whole ship to hear. He even sounded proud of it and not the least bit guilty. I wanted to blurt out that I had never seen Arturo before in my life but somehow I knew the captain wasn't going to believe me.

"Explain yourself, seaman," I heard the captain say to him.

Arturo's voice betrayed that he was resigned to whatever fate held in store for him but nonetheless sought to make my case as best as he could. "The boy's come a long way to find his family," he began.

Inexplicably, he began to extol my virtues as an aspiring sailor, almost making it sound as if I were already an integral part of the ship's crew. "You should have seen him below deck, sir," he said. "He was very—"

"If I had seen him at all, he wouldn't have made it <u>this</u> far," the captain snapped. He brusquely turned his attention back to me. "Does your family know where you are?"

My answer really wasn't a lie. "Yes," I replied. Hadn't Mrs. Scarpetti herself said that when people die they still stay close to you forever? If Mama, Papa and Gina were looking down from heaven, they knew exactly where I was…and why.

"He has an uncle in New York—" Arturo started to add but the captain shot him a withering glare.

"It's true," I eagerly chimed in, foolishly thinking my participation at this juncture would be useful. "He lives in New York and his name is—"

"I think I've heard enough," the captain said, his face a stony visage that projected no compassion. "As soon as we reach port, you'll be turned over to Immigration and deported back to wherever the hell you came from."

Anguish almost overcame the last shreds of my control, my throat aching with defeat. It couldn't end like this, not when I'd come so far! I looked to Arturo but his head was bent down. Whatever spark of hope had lingered for me in these final days was cruelly extinguished by the captain's words.

As he started to turn away, I found the voice to ask him one last question. "I have a suitcase in the cabin…Arturo's cabin," I said, adding a respectful "sir" to the end in the vain hope he might be impressed by my manners. "May I have it back, please?" If I was going to be sent home, it wasn't going to be without my clothes and my pictures of my family.

His reply, when it came, was cold and exact. "Nothing below deck was salvageable," he informed me. As he strode off, it occurred to me that he hadn't even said he was sorry.

It also occurred to me that I had lost even more than my clothes and the pictures. I had lost the leather pocketbook containing all my money.

* * *

Was there no end to the questions?! The two men in suits who came aboard to take me away kept me alone in a room on the ship. Each time I answered a question, they'd ask me another one and then another after that. Weren't my answers good enough for them? The only question I wanted to ask was how I was going to reach my goal if they weren't going to let me stay. Clearly, they didn't think that was their problem.

When they finally escorted me off the ship, I anxiously looked around for Arturo but he was nowhere in sight. Had men been questioning him, too? I hoped things wouldn't go too hard on him. After all, he was the ship's cook. What would the crew eat if he weren't around to fix meals for them?

I was taken to a detention room where people of all nationalities huddled in small groups. Had they also been stowaways? Some of them were crying, others were looking defiant and pacing the floor. Still others sat staring into space, lost in the thought of dreams that – like mine – weren't ever going to come true. I found a corner and curled up in it, bewildered as to why God was putting me through so much agony. "Please don't leave me now," I prayed. "Please don't stop protecting me…"

I waited in that crowded room for an hour. Then I was called into a different room to endure yet another round of interrogation. There was a new person this time along with the two I had already met. They had also brought a judge and an interpreter who asked me if I'd feel more comfortable talking in Italian. For two more hours they asked questions - repeating some, rephrasing others, unbalancing me, making me uncomfortable and infinitely sadder. I was lost. I knew I was lost. Finally, at the end of it the judge told me I was going to be deported. I nodded my understanding.

They handed me over to another man who spoke pretty good Italian and who was to be in charge of taking me to a compound where I'd spend the night before being sent back home. "What did you do to get deported?" he asked in curiosity. I saw no harm in telling him the whole story. He seemed nice enough. He also asked me if I liked ice cream and bought each of us a cone.

He listened sympathetically as I told him everything from beginning to end. "So close but still so far," he murmured when I was through.

"I bet I could have found him," I said. It was a moot point, of course, the irony being that Uncle Alfredo would now be none the wiser that I had ever been in town.

"I bet you could, too," he said. "You're a pretty smart kid."

And then he reached into his vest pocket, pulled out his wallet, and handed me two American bills. "That's ten dollars," he said.

I looked at them with detachment and started to hand them back. "They're yours to spend," he explained.

I didn't understand.

"In 30 minutes," he replied, "I'm going to report that you got away from me. I wish I could give you more…"

I wasn't sure whether he meant more money or more time. Nor was I sure why he even wanted to help me.

He smiled. "America is all about dreamers, Corrado," he said. "If we sent everyone home just because they're from somewhere else –" He chuckled as if enjoying a private joke. He looked at his watch. "If you're going to go find that uncle of yours, there's no sense delaying it any longer."

I didn't move at first, too stunned to let the enormity of his words sink in. And then I jumped to my feet, not sure if I should shake his hand, give him a hug or just run out the door with a wave. I never looked back to see how long he watched me. I only knew for the moment that God had resumed watching me and that I had one last chance to make good on the promise I'd made to myself.

* * *

I remembered from Papa's stories that New York had a place called Little Italy. With a confidence that belied my inner quaking, I got a taxicab driver to take me there, not daring to walk on dark streets in a strange city by myself.

"What address?" he gruffly asked.

Address? I pretended I'd forgotten the exact number but that I was sure I'd recognize it when I saw it. My plan, of course, was to point to the first Italian restaurant we came across and happily hop out as if I were meeting someone.

His eyes caught mine in the rearview mirror. "You been to the Italian Club?" he asked.

It sounded festive, not to mention a promising place to start my search. "The one in Little Italy?" I inquired just in case there happened to be more than one.

He grunted something unintelligible in response as he navigated his vehicle down what had to be one of the busiest city streets I'd ever seen.

I was really here! I still couldn't believe it. I was still daunted, of course, by the enormity of it and Mrs. Scarpetti's observation that finding anyone in a place this huge was like looking for a needle in a haystack.

The taxicab eased to a stop in front of the Italian Club. "How much?" I asked, trying to sound as if I had been riding around in taxicabs all my life.

The driver's reply made my mouth drop open. "Five dollars?!" I gasped.

He turned around in the seat and repeated it. His demeanor intimidated me and for a split second I wondered how far I'd get if I bolted from the backseat before he could get tout of the front. I realized I was already in enough trouble. What harm would a little more do?

There were several couples standing outside

the club and smoking cigarettes, though, and I wasn't
sure if some of the men might decide to chase me if
I ran. I reached into my pocket to remove one of the
two bills. The driver took it from me, then stared at
me as if in expectation of more.

"It's five dollars, yes?" I said, hoping I hadn't
misheard him.

With a snort, he turned back to the steering
wheel and waited for me to let myself out.

I started toward the door but one of the
gentlemen who was smoking told me that the club
was closing in 15 minutes.

"Oh, I'm just looking for someone," I said.

"You're a little young, aren't you?" the man's
lady friend said to me.

I politely informed her that I would be 16
next year.

The man and his wife chuckled and were soon
joined by another couple. "Who is it you're looking
for?" the second lady asked.

I gave them my uncle's name. None of them, however, knew who he was. An older, well dressed gentleman had now stepped out and asked me in Italian where I was originally from. He clapped his hands in delight when I told him. His own family, he said, had emigrated from Lessante before the war. "Where are you staying?" he wanted to know. Before I realized it, a small crowd had gathered around me, murmuring their concern when I told them that I had lost all of my belongings on the ocean crossing.

"I have a friend in the State Department," one of the men jovially volunteered. "We could get you duplicates of your papers in no time at all."

My nerves tensed immediately. Here I was among my own people and the threat was already looming that I'd be exposed as an illegal immigrant.

The older man remarked that he and his wife had a house just down the street. "There's plenty of room," he said.

"Plenty of room for what?" his wife inquired

as she joined the group.

He enthusiastically related to her that I was from Lessante and at once she began asking me about various families she knew.

"You're tiring the boy out," he interrupted her. "There'll be time enough in the morning to ask him your questions…"

The next thing I knew, a taxicab pulled up and the three of us crowded into the backseat. I noted with a sigh of relief that it was not the same driver who had deposited me.

"What fun!" the wife said when her husband told her that I was looking for my uncle. She reminded him that he knew lots of people and that it shouldn't be too hard to find the one I was looking for. He didn't sound as convinced to me as she did but I was also exhausted and could happily have slept in the taxicab, content to be lulled to sleep by the sound of my own language.

* * *

I didn't know what Mr. Lagomarsino's trade was but he had obviously done well for himself. His wife had also laid out some clothes that she said their nephew had left behind on his last visit. The pants were a little long but I rolled up the cuffs, not really minding that it probably wasn't fashionable. As I stated to pull on my shoes, something wet and clumpy fell out. I didn't recognize it at first. It was the lira I had so carefully stuffed into the toe when I left Lessante. Obviously my shipboard experience during the fire had permanently rendered it worthless.

I sat on the edge of the bed in the Lagomarsino's frilly guest room and took stock of my situation. I had five American dollars to my name, I had no identity (as far as the United States was concerned) and an uncle somewhere in New York who didn't even know I was here. What scared me the most, though, was that the English I knew could only take me so far. What little, full-time exposure I had to it was that it was too fast and that I could only grab hold of every third word. I caught myself realizing that these were the very same things my uncle had faced when he came here. He, too, had been as alone as I was. The singular difference was that he had been older and had proper paperwork when he came so as not to label him a wanted man. I thought of the stories I read about the American West. Even now, I wondered, was a poor sketch of my face being posted in public places throughout the city? Would the Lagomarsinos see it and turn me in for a reward?

Even as I went down to breakfast, I half-expected to see the men from the Immigration Department waiting for me. Instead, it was only Mrs. Lagomarsino and her husband having coffee. "Would you like some, Corrado?" she offered.

"Yes, thank you," I said, glancing at the fresh fruit and rolls that I could have devoured in a single bite.

Mr. Lagomarsino asked me to tell him about my uncle. "It was so late last night," he apologized. "I may have missed something…"

How many times had I told this story, I thought. If I counted my experience with the immigration people, it was probably close to a million.

"Have you ever met him?" Mr. Lagomarsino – Tony – wanted to know.

I shook my head and related that I had been very young when Uncle Alfredo left for America.

"What was his last name again, dear?" Mrs. Lagomarsino asked me.

"Gordini. Alfredo Gordini."

She looked at her husband who, in turn, looked at me. "I know your uncle, Corrado," he said. "I know him well."

Why hadn't he said so last night?! My mind spun. Maybe it was a mistake. Maybe he hadn't heard me correctly. "Alfredo Gordini," I repeated. "Is that the man you know?"

There was a long pause. "We do occasional business," he said. "I have known your uncle since childhood."

Did it mean that he had known my father as well? I wanted to ask but I dared not interrupt Mr. Lagomarsino's answer.

"It was sheer luck finding him when he came here," he continued. He chuckled. "Although it's not exactly hard to find Italians in New York..."

I didn't know what to say. I wanted to laugh. I wanted to cry. The latter, perhaps, more than anything except that it was for joy. Mrs. Lagomarsino stood up and came over to cradle me. "It's all right," she said.

She didn't have to tell me that. I already knew it was true.

"He's getting married," her husband told me. "Very soon, I think." He went on to tell me that a friend of his had offered Uncle Alfredo a job as a painter in Buffalo and that he had done well. "People like him," he said. "He has a good personality and knows how to please."

"Is he still there?" I asked. "In Buffalo?" I didn't know where that was but at least I knew that he was still alive.

Mr. Lagomarsino nodded. "He rented a furnished room. He worked hard. When he met Laura – the lady he's marrying – life was complete for him."

It would be even more complete, I thought, when he discovered that his brother's son had come all the way to New York to find him.

Laura, my host went on, was Italian-American. His wife added that she was tall and slender with long dark hair and blue eyes. She worked at a little diner that Alfredo considered his home-away-from-home. Her parents, Mrs. Lagomarsino told me, were from Naples. Their only reservation about a courtship was the difference in their ages. Laura was a widow whose husband had died of a heart attack. "It was love at first sight," she said, beaming.

The same, however, could not be said for Alfredo. Who could blame a man who was once so bitterly betrayed by the only woman he swore to love forever? Laura, they told me, had put a lot of pressure on Alfredo for marriage. And finally, now, they were engaged to be married in less than two months time.

I wanted to know how he had explained his first wife to her. The Lagomarsinos exchanged a brief glance, no doubt thinking me much too inquisitive for one who had not yet achieved adulthood. "It wasn't easy, to be sure," Mrs. Lagomarsino said. "He waited until her parents came for dinner and – over wine - confessed to the damage that had been done to him." To my uncle's surprise, the family accepted him and the indignities he had overcome and began to prepare for a wedding.

"I haven't heard from him in months, though," Tony regretfully admitted. "He would talk to me about Laura all the time when they first met.

His engagement, sadly, I had to hear about from someone else."

I eagerly asked if he knew how to reach him.

"No," he replied, "but I believe it can be done through the friend of a friend."

I couldn't sleep at all that night, knowing that the wheels of action had been set in motion. Tony had gone to the Italian club after work as was his usual custom. That night was a little different though, as he was on a mission. He questioned everyone and anyone about my uncle's whereabouts. Many people had seen him between Brooklyn and Buffalo but no one knew how to reach him. But that day it turned out not to matter.

"Tony, phone for you!" shouted the bartender.

He assumed it was his wife asking him to pick up something on the way home. He nearly dropped the phone when he heard who was on the end of the line.

"Tony? Tony, it's Alfredo! I knew I'd find

you at the club. I didn't even try you at home first."

"I was speechless when I heard his voice," Mr. Lagomarsino told us as soon as he came home.

I was on pins and needles, unable to believe this good fortune. "What did he say?" I wanted to know.

Excitedly, he repeated the conversation word for word. Alfredo was getting married to Laura and wanted Tony to be his best man.

"What did you say?" his wife asked.

"I told him his nephew was here," he replied.

"No, no, not about that," she said, forgetting for a moment that I was there. "What about the wedding?" Mrs. Lagomarsino, I had learned, lived for the social scene.

"Yes, yes, of course, I agreed," he replied.

I cut in to ask what he said when Mr. Lagomarsino told him about me.

"He was surprised, of course. More than surprised I think."

Why did I have the sinking feeling this wasn't going to go exactly the way I wanted it to?

"Why are you doing this to me?" he asked me. Mr. Lagomarsino awkwardly continued, "He had heard about the accident but had been told by someone – I don't know who – that all of you had died."

I felt all the color drain from my face. "He didn't know I was still alive."

Mr. Lagomarsino shook his head. "It took some convincing to tell him that you were the only one to make it out alive."

There hovered a long silence in the room that even the talkative Mrs. Lagomarsino dared not break.

"He'd like to talk to you," Mr. Lagomarsino said. "I told him that he could call here tomorrow."

Tomorrow? An eternity! I can't even remember what we ate for dinner that night or anything that we talked about. I only knew that tomorrow couldn't come fast enough.

* * *

I heard the telephone as soon as it rang. I heard Mr. Lagomarsino say a few words and then call out my name. "He wants to talk to you," he said, holding out the receiver. I nervously took it in both hands, imagining that if I dropped it the connection would be lost forever.

"Hello?"

My uncle began to sob when he heard my voice. "Corrado?" he said. "Corrado, is it really you?"

✳ ✳ ✳

The drive to Buffalo the next morning seemed interminable. I tried to distract myself with the sights I'd never seen and Tony tried to keep me busy with chit-chat that he knew I wasn't paying any attention to.

I was almost there!

I think I like the way my Uncle Alfredo tells the story best. He says when the car drove into his driveway, Laura grabbed his hand and the two of them stepped off the porch, ready for me. When I climbed out of the car, he said, he knew his brother didn't really die. He knew his soul would be at ease finally, knowing I was safe, but that through me he was still right here. He hugged me, kissed me, and everyone cried. And when he finally found words for me, he said, "Your strength, your courage, your determination… you remind me so very much of your father."

And that, I tell anyone who will listen, will always be my favorite part of the story.

Epilogue – The Back Story

A Sicilian family fled to the mountains as the Mediterranean coast was pummeled in July of 1943. As the family sought safe cover, they realized one of them was missing. Luigi, the father, ran quickly back to Pozzallo, a small Sicilian town, to find their home in ruins.

Few walls and just a fraction of the ceiling remained. That piece of ceiling was holding up a baby hammock, where family lore has it, the baby continued to sleep peacefully. Two years old at the time, Corrado Ammatuna was not meant that day to be a casualty.

At 15, he left his home and began working on a cruise ship. Over the next two years he would work on cruise ships and oil tankers visiting many parts of the world. He sent home whatever money he could. Docked in New York, he decided he wouldn't be on the return voyage. He knew he was destined to live his own American dream.

Corrado hustled and quickly found work where he met Angelo Costa. He became close to Costa, so close in fact that Corrado considered him to be like a father. Costa taught Corrado about manufacturing. And too he taught him how to navigate through life. Corrado moved to California and became a proud citizen of the United States. Hard work propelled his career and he became head of several machine shops in the San Jose and Sacramento areas.

As he sent his youngest off to college, he was stricken with Mesothelioma, a rare cancer. Faced with the hardship of disease, his faith and determination never wavered. Corrado managed to put others before himself, just as he had done all his life.

Someone like Corrado only comes along every so often and to be a part of his life is something that all who knew him treasured. His many stories could make you laugh, learn, cry, and they always made you feel loved. I know because he was my Dad.

As his days grew numbered and the Doctors could do little more our family planned and went on a cruise. We all knew it was to be his final trip with us. Dad was as sick as he had ever been, still he was able to endure the plane ride and start his vacation at sea with his family. Though he didn't seem able to do too much, he made sure we all had a good time and took in as much as possible.

It was the cruise's formal night. The night everyone dresses up, attends a special dinner, and has photos taken. Even with the disease taking a toll on his appearance, Dad looked sharp in his tuxedo. He mustered the strength to savor a few bites of steak. The flashing lights of cameras shined on him and his family that night as the ships photo crew made a record of the special occasion. He knew this was his grand exit.

As the evening drew to its end, he retired

to his room, lay down and waited his time.   He was restful, calm and happy. He had completed his mission in life. He knew he had done well. His wife and three children loved him, and now his time had come to an end.

His end to this life came peacefully and quietly.

Carlo Giuliano Ammatuna